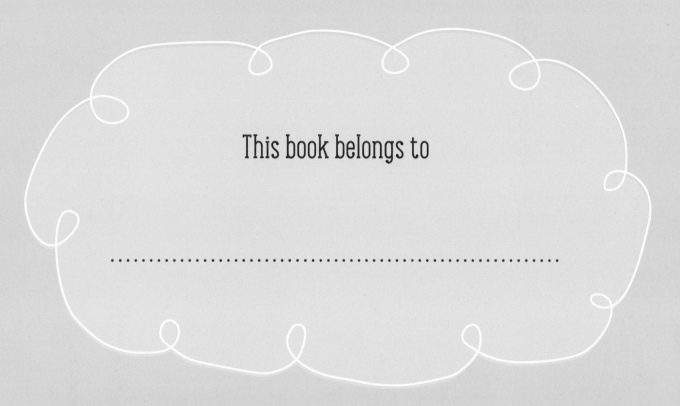

This book belongs to

....

Written by Rosie Greening.
Illustrated by Lara Ede.

The Sugar Plum Fairy's Wand

Lara Ede ✱ Rosie Greening

make
believe
ideas

On **Christmas Eve**, old Grandpa Ted
brought gifts for Clare and Little Fred.

"**Me first, me first!**" cried Fred with glee,
and tore his open **eagerly.**

Inside, he found a man in red.
"The **nutcracker!**" his grandpa said.
"He's from a kingdom far from here
that's full of **snow** and **Christmas cheer.**"

Clare's parcel had a **doll** inside.
"The **Sugar Plum Fairy!**" Grandpa cried.
"Her wand makes yummy gingerbread –
your favourite Christmas **treat**," he said.

"My toy's the BEST,"
said Little Fred.

"I like mine MORE!"
his sister said.

They **thanked** old Ted, then rushed away –
the pair could hardly wait to **play!**

Clare said to Fred, "Now let's **pretend**
our toys are **real** and we're all friends."
And so the pair began to weave
a magic world of **MAKE-BELIEVE.**

They dreamt up **lands** of luscious sweets,
of sparkling snow and Christmas **treats**.
But soon, they had to **sleep** instead,
so Clare and Fred went up to bed.

When Clare woke up, to her **surprise,**
her fairy doll had **grown** in size!

"I've **lost** my wand," the fairy said,
"and now I **can't make** gingerbread!"

She sighed, "No Christmas is **complete**
without my yummy festive treats.
But only my **wand** can do the trick –
I need some help to find it **quick!**"

"I'll **help!**" Clare told her with a grin,
and then her room began to **spin**.

Big **icy trees** began to **grow,**
and soon the **floor** was crunchy **SNOW!**

The fairy looked around with **pride**.
"We're in the **LAND OF SNOW**," she cried.
"Let's **skate** across the frozen pond
and see if we can find my **wand**."

They **searched** the land, but couldn't see
just where the fairy's **wand** might be.
And so they made a sign instead:

PLEASE HELP US FIND THIS WAND!   it said.

A passing snowman gave a **SHOUT**:
"I've **seen** that wand, without a doubt!
Somebody had it yesterday –
I think he **ran off** thataway!"

LAND OF SWEETS

The **kindly fairy** took Clare's hand.
"We're going to another land."
And in a **FLASH** of coloured light,
the **Land of Sweets** swirled into sight.

This place looked **good** enough to eat,
with milkshake streams and piles of **TREATS**.
"My wand only makes **gingerbread** –
let's **look** for some," the fairy said.

They **hurried** through the toffee trees that showered **sprinkles** in the breeze.

And soon they found a **sugar mouse**, collecting **crumbs** outside his house.

He **STAMPED** his paw and gave a squeak.
"My housework's going to take **all week!**"

"The forest's full of **gingerbread**:
the crumbs are **EVERYWHERE!**" he said.

"IT **MUST** HAVE BEEN YOUR **WAND**," Clare cried.
"This **trail** of crumbs can be our guide."

So off they went, at quite a pace,
until they reached a **fireplace**.

They hurried through, and what a **sight** –
a land of **tinsel, gifts** and **light!**
Clare gazed at all the twinkling trees.
"It's **CHRISTMAS LAND!**" she cried with glee.

At last, they **spied** someone ahead.
"**THE NUTCRACKER!**" the fairy said.

"But you're my **friend** –
why would you take
the magic wand I use to bake?"

The nutcracker turned very **red**.
"I can **explain**," he shyly said.
"I stole your magic wand away
to make your **GIFT** for Christmas Day."

"You see," he said, "I **longed** to make a castle built from yummy cake."

"But I've got **no more** gingerbread, and now I'm out of **TIME**," he said.

The fairy smiled, "I **understand**.
And now we're here, I'll lend a hand."

She **waved** her wand around the treats...

and soon the castle was **complete!**

The nutcracker said, "It looks **divine!**
I hope you like this **gift** of mine.
I know taking your wand was wrong,
but I have **loved you** for so long."

"I love you too!" the fairy said,
and smiled up at the man in red.

Then in a **FLASH** and with a **BOOM**,
Clare found herself back in her **room**.

When Clare **woke up,** she looked around.
Her two new friends could not be **found**.
"I must have dreamt it all," she said,
and went to find her brother, Fred.

She found him by the Christmas tree,
unwrapping presents happily.
"Look at the table," Fred declared.

So off she ran,
then stopped and **stared**.

A **castle** made of gingerbread
was on the table next to Fred.

Two little dolls were tucked inside:
the **NUTCRACKER** and his new **BRIDE!**

But as Clare **leaned** in close, she saw
this **note** stuck to the tiny door: